AN ELIXIR OF LOVE

SHYAM KESHARIYA

First Published in July 2020

Published By:
Kalon Maple Publishing
+91 9665 609 444

ISBN: 978-81-946591-6-7
Price: 219₹

Layout Design, Cover Design & Illustration:
Mrunaal Gawhande

Distributed by:
Paperback: amazon.com, amazon.in, flipkart, kalonmaplepublishing.com
E-Book: amazon.in/com, apple (ibooks stores in 51 countries), barnes & noble (us and uk), scribd, kobo, and blio, overdrive (world's largest library ebook platform serving 20,000 + libraries), baker & taylor axis 360, tolino, gardners (askews & holts and browns books for students), bibliotheca cloud library (3,000 public libraries) and odilo (2,100 public libraries in north america, south america and europe) + paperback

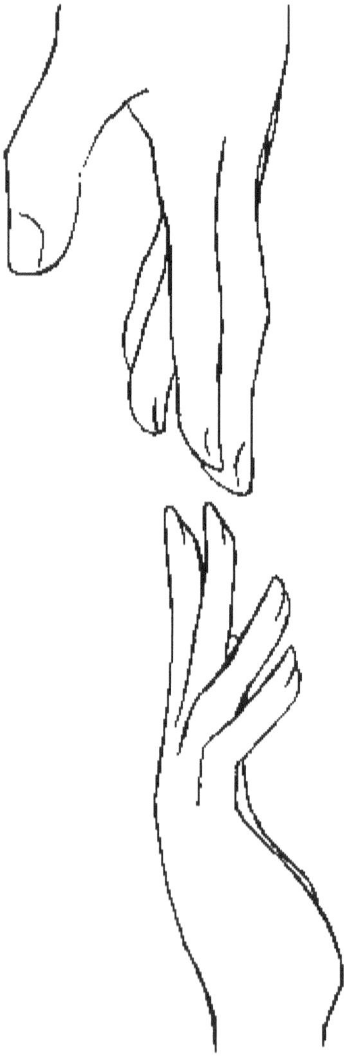

To my Dad and Mom, who gave me this Life.
To my sister, who defined life for me.
To my Family and Friends, who became a part of my Life.
To all my supporters who love my work, without whom this book would have been incomplete.
To the team I never met but was associated with the completion of the Book.
To all those souls who love me more than anything and will do.

Publisher's Note:

"An Elixir of Love" is a collaboration of different feelings penned in a single book, when Shyam came to me with an idea of making a book of poetry and when he sent me his manuscript, I thought the book had everything and you can read the book in any mood, right from the cover to the interior of the book we wanted the book to be the masterpiece, with the help of our team we were able to do that, Shyam is an aspiring writer and I was happy to head start his writing journey.

This book isn't just a book of poems it has meaningful prose, dedication letters and all the normal feeling that we feel every day in day to day life expressed in poetic and blissful way. This book is surely going to win many hearts.

If you are a poetry reader then you know that the poems hits differently to everyone and what will be better than reading a book whose meaning will be different for all of us. Shyam and I discussed some different unique writing patterns and for this book we made sure that we use these techniques.

Shyam has potential to pen any feeling in a very smooth way with that he explains his words with some unique examples, "An Elixir of Love" became the title when few more titles too were in the race.

In the month of March we were on the verge of making the book online but some natural disasters made us wait until we get any favorable time.

Shyam and I both agreed, as we wanted the book to reach all the places without any hurdles and believe me since then our writer here has become impatient and is becoming stubborn to make it available like in minutes. Well jokes apart but the book deserves to be read by everyone and hence we finally present to you this book who has seen many ups and down but have made it all the way to your hearts, my heart.

Enjoy book with some remarkable visuals and feel every word of it. I wish this book and Shyam all the best!

-Mrunaal Gawhande
(Founder – Kalon Maple Publishing)

ACKNOWLEDGEMENT

This book holds a place in my heart, not only because it's my first book but because it's something which I will be gifting my parents on my 20th Birthday. Just to thank them for all the hard work and love they have given me, a book from me to them, to make them feel proud. I would love to mention their name here, Kaushik Keshriya & Shilpa Keshariya.

I would love to thank my sister, Hiteksha Keshariya. For all the efforts and support, she has given me.

I would like to thank my Grandparents and my family members for always having faith in me and my dreams.

I would like to acknowledge Rohan Mehta, Yash Dave, Nirmal Shah, Rahul Dhruv, Sahil Vairagi and Varun Pal for the courage and optimism they have given me.

I also want to appreciate Krishna Oza, Jinal Sedani, Anjali Jadeja, Amy Desai and Khushi Butani for keeping me motivated and bringing the best out of me.

Heartfelt thanks to my inner circle and the people whose support brought me here, publishing my first book. Thank you all.

A big thanks to my teacher Kinjal Mehta, Dipak Dave, Amit Pandey and Vidhi Mehta for their support.

A special thanks to Mrunaal Gawhande and my entire publishing team from Kalon Maple Publishing

Last but not the least; I would like to thank the Almighty God for always showing me the path and having these blessings upon me.

AN ELIXIR OF LOVE

What an amazing feeling it is, to love you with all my heart,
To realize how important you are, being my life's part.

And to holding you in my arms, kissing your forehead,
Love had me whole, making me happy and even sad.

And to live the real joy of life with your name on every beat,
Which is inseparable, alike ground under our feet!

This was love, making me crazy, my forever kind of feel,
Looking in your eyes, I felt home as heart started to heal.

A vibe beyond every word said, but not beyond silence,
Because not everything felt can be said or wrote with pen.

Something felt with heart, a connection so pure than truth,
Having access over everything, over Anger, Pain and Ruth!

Making it the strongest bond, to show the world its power,
By winning every fight and with that there is love, a glower.

Shining in the sky with wings to fly just like bats and dove,
Maybe all this just because we had "AN ELIXIR OF LOVE"

Content

PHILIA

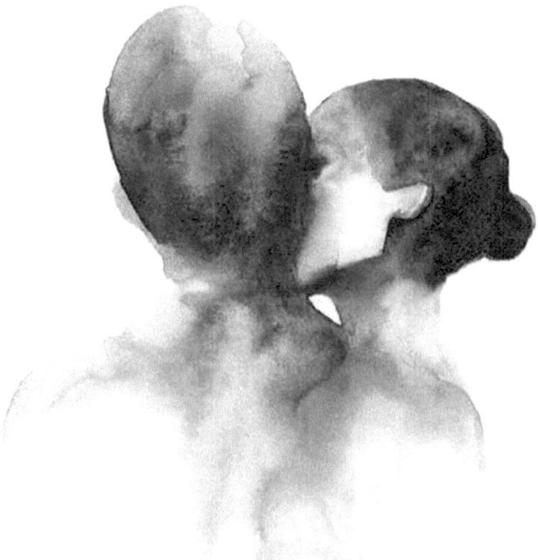

"Every writing defines a story which needs to be heard."

She wrote
“His Queen” on her Instagram Bio
"Her king"
Read his tombstone.

His love for her kept on multiplying
All he wanted was
-she shan't give him a reason
to get it multiplied by zero.

Not every love story has to be of a boy and a girl
some love stories can be different.

We value a watch
as much as we value sages.
Because we bow down to both,
when we see them.
Hence they pursue equal values in our life.

A clock and a compass both have a pointer which rotates. The only difference is that clock moves on its own. While compass moves by our choice. So we can't have control over time but we can have a control over where we want to reach. So you have to decide, what you want to live life with!

I didn't want to spend my life between books.
All I want was life between pages of a passport.

Rays of sun
travel such a long distance
still shines
then how can you shine your life
just by being at one place?

2 Eyes for crying,
but 32 teeth for smiling!
Overcome your sadness with happiness,
it is 16 times greater!

Among all those colors on my face,
the one which made my face glow was the color of her love!

It's always better to believe in Faith than Fate.
At least you have the power to do something new!

She thought her attraction was love
and I thought my love was her life
and that's how my heart broke.

There is a magic called 'Your smile'
which makes my heart happy.

"So you proposed her?"
asked his best friend,

"I don't need to propose myself!"
replied a true lover!

How weird the journey of life goes!
When I came to this world,
I began with crying.
While I end up with living,
People would cry for me.
The life cycle goes the same
but situations differ.

PRAGMA

For walking,
we need 2 legs.
When we travel in a train,
it runs on 2 tracks.
Even the crippled ones,
needs a wheel chair with 2 wheels,
because life isn't fair without a pair.

They shared the chocolate, she did keep the wrapper. Not because he gave it, it was because she believed in their love, alike chocolate they would share every little thing in their life. So the chocolate became their sweet head start of their endless journey of love!

I always thought that they are my dreams, I have to fulfill them. But I always had someone by my side, who worked along with me, to fulfill my dreams, to achieve my goals. He tried hard, for my dreams, he worked more, for my dreams, he was even disappointed, more than me, when we faced failure, yet he stood up and tried harder. Later I realized, "My dreams" were "Our dreams". And he was none other than my Dad.

I guess climbing the jumping castle was much easier and fun than climbing the castle of life.

I write because I secretly want to tell her all the things which she doesn't know!

Graveyard is the only place where you will find true love because only the people who really care and love visits' it.

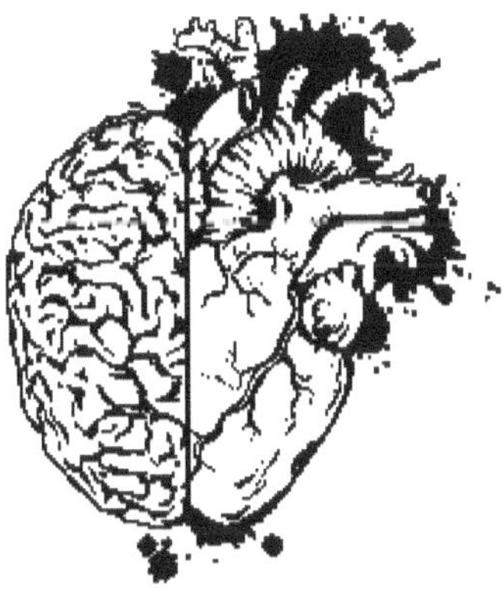

People say that things only shine when it's dark but also remember that sun shines too! People worship the sun everyday not the moon!

Similarly, your love for her would be shining brightly but it's in the dark and she is someone who worship's a love of bright day while your love will never be seen unless it's night!

The flame of our first candle light dinner, converted into the holy fire when we married and then burning us into ashes so that we would reunite back in heaven! With every increment in fire our journey increased from one stage to another and so did our love and commitments.

As the Darkness hides everything,

I want to hide you from the world, because you are the only one, who light's my life out of Darkness!

Every day looking at my shoes, I wondered when will I find someone who would walk with me in the journey of life?

Attraction is always towards a specific thing like smile, eyes etc. While love is beyond everything, it cannot be pointed out like attraction.

Attraction is just a drop of "The Ocean of Love."

When you start falling for your friend, the mind enters in a subconscious situation and the heart stands on hold! It can't decide whether continue the never ending process of falling in love with her or to bury everything that you feel for her.

If you still love her?
Then why are you with someone else?

My love for her is going to last forever, but I can't resist the people who truly love me as people whom I love don’t care about me. So I can't do injustice with the people who do!

I wish stopping time was possible,
at the least I could have got the time to hold myself!

I wish
pain killers could also stop the pain
from which the heart suffered.

STORGE

A LIFE PARTNER

Have you ever felt that life is too long? Have you ever heard people saying that life is too short? Yes, it's true; we never know when it's going to end. So find someone in life that makes your life clear, supports you and is independent. We have seen many people wearing glasses. We know why they wear it. It's their basic requirement to see clearly. It makes their vision clear. Similarly, we should find our life partner who makes our vision of life clear. The one who is always there for us, till the end of everything and beyond it. One who is always there to protect us just like the glasses protects' our eyes. On the other side there are few people who are completely blind. Those who live their life with white cane (walking stick). It is their basic need, as they can't see anything but still live their entire life by its support. Similarly, our Life Partner should always be there to support us, in each stage of Life. And the ones, who neither have glasses nor they are Blind. They live their life independently. Similarly, our partner should have faith in us and should be independent.

So find someone with all these qualities for life, I'm sure you would not feel life boundless.

WEAK

I am weak,
when I know I'm on the wrong path but still I cannot leave it.

I am weak,
when people tell me to say things which can hurt someone.

I am weak,
when my lips can't tell the words which my heart wants to express.

I am weak,
when things start to go in a situation where I know
I will go through worst.

I am weak,
because I am and it's not that every time you have to be strong.

You can make things better sometimes by being weak.

RAIN

Look how life has been! I saw some kids making boats to float and I could see my childhood. We all made boats, every time it rained. Looking to those boats I realized, I remembered every folding of paper just like every folding of childhood! It took time and hard work to build those boats and so did to make childhood memories! But once the boat was on water, it just floated and went through the journey where water took it. I guess that's how our childhood went by, at the same flow; we never knew where it would lead us. Those moments will find you happiness and cherish life the way it passes by.

A Coin has two Sides

It's about how you want to live your life! A coin has two sides and it's used for tossing. They always look, what's there on the top? While sometimes it's good to look the lower side as well and see the pain, difficulties and should try to learn from it that no matter how many times it loses still it keeps on being part of the game. Going deeper we can further come to a conclusion that the side that won could have never won if the other side wasn't there. As no matter how much good you are, you always need a partner in life and have to be ready for the loss that both of you are going to face. But we should still participate in it because when one side loses, gives a standing ovation to the other side being it's back to show the entire world that life has both winning and losing. It's just that people never understand it. They never take the advantage and live the life to the fullest with what they have at the moment and try to go for something which has lesser possibilities of being there. I personally think we should be happy with what we have and live the way with whatever our life gives us. As loss is going to come for sure but facing them happily and wisely is more important. And the best part I love about being deprived of is when you get to know how much it valued and gives you an advice how to be better then. So not all that matters in life is what you did. All that matters is did you have a happy life and was it so virtuous. And most important is to always appreciate your partner, as they were there with you in all your success and failures.

A ROLE OF A FORK AND A SPOON

I am sure that everyone has dreamt something for themselves and it would be something which would make them happy in Life. Here I am going to tell you about a spoon and a fork. We all have used both and we are very much familiar with them. We know that when we want to grab something such as french fries, noodles, etc. We use fork as it is something which we cannot take a lot at once and we cannot even use a spoon in it as it is not as sharp as fork. Similarly, in life when we want to achieve our goals we have to make ourselves sharp enough so we can fulfill each dream one by one. That does not mean that spoon is of no use. Of course it is, every time we have rice we use it and at that place fork is useless. So spoon is useful but where in our life? It is useful in the times when we need happiness in daily basis just like we eat rice daily. So spoon shows that it does not differentiate anything. In the same way we should not differentiate happiness with other individuals. People hold some importance in life and all are responsible for some sort of happiness in our life. So be smart enough and use spoon and fork at the right places.

LACE

We always have seen and said that a shoe is useless without its pair. They always should be in a pair but have we ever thought that even lace needs to be in pair. When we tie them we always make sure that it's tight so we tie it properly, sometimes when it gets loose we open it and tie it again. A lace goes through many holes and changes its path but at last it does get tied with the other end. Similarly why don't we do the same with relations? In situations where the bond starts becoming loose and we do nothing to save it until it gets worse instead of making that bond tight again. A shoe is useless without its pair, so is a lace and so is our life. The only difference is that lace and shoes come in a perfect pair while we have to find the one right for us, the one who makes our match perfect. Every lace gets tied uncountable times but still it forms the same beautiful pattern when we tie it. We do need to find for our other half and when we do, I'm sure we all will be able to form the beautiful pattern in life as well.

NOT JUST A SORRY

I know "Sorry" means nothing these days but for me it still means the same, not repeating the mistakes which I did. A word which can bind people back together, who were about to leave or the one who left! A word with a capability to give a chance, to change ourselves. A word to tell to those, we can't bear losing. A word defining that there is a light of goodness and hope that believes that people can be better if they will. It's not just any word, it's an emotion. It defines a lot of things like please take my apology into consideration, it won't happen again and it even means please don't leave because you mean a lot to me.

WHAT YOU REALLY FEEL IS LOVE?

When you will be in true love, you will always do what's good for him/her. No matter what he/she does to you! You will never think bad of him/her. You will have the strength to accept all his/her mistakes and you will know that it was his/her mistake and you will be ready to pay for his/her punishments, this is love.

Now, if you need someone at any cost. You want him/her to be with you for rest of your life. If you protect him/her even in her mistakes and you do not let anyone punish him/her. Instead you will get angry on the person who will be trying to punish him/her. If you want him/her just to be with you and no one else, then it's POSSESSION.

Now, if you find someone really attractive and you feel like he/she is the one, who is meant to be with you. Finally, when he/she will actually be with you or he/she will be ready to be with you and you feel like this is it! It wasn't expected to be this way and if you are scared of all the responsibilities you have to take of him/her then it's INFATUATION.

Now, if you like your friends praising him/her and about his/her work or something. You want him/her to be proud having you. You think keeping him/her happy is all that matters. No one is as important as he/she is to you. You think of giving him/her anything he/she wants. You will do anything, even the wrong to be with him/her. You will not care whether it's right or wrong. For you only he/she will matter, then it's TEMPTATION.

As love has the power to free you from him/her and the world. Love is something which will not need any trust. It will have boundaries but will never hold you back to stay with him/her, love makes a connection with your own heart and if it's true, then there will be one heart and one soul between two bodies. That will make you love yourself. So it will never matter if he/she is with you or even if he/she isn't, that is what I call LOVE.

BEST JOURNEY OF LIFE

MEMORIES! Not just a word, it has the ability to bring happiness and sorrow at the same time. It's not just about the moments; it's the people who make it special. Remembering, laughing and wishing to live them again. It not only has a special place in heart but the heart still beats just to have all those time again with the FRIENDS who came and never left. Friendship day isn't just about exchanging belts; it's a promise from a friend to another to be with him/her till the end. Some Friendship does not last forever, because as "Friendship" itself has "Ship", it's a journey which we start with some mates who later becomes a part of family. Some ships does sink but some ends at HEAVEN, crossing the ocean of life. All we need is our friends as crew of the ship and memories which we built with them as fuel. It is one of the best journey on which a person can go.

BE MY HOME

Every time when I see those lovely brown eyes,
I see a home for my soul and pure love without lies.

Watching all your madness, I could feel true happiness,
A home where a smile made it all shine over the face.

All your imperfections started being so perfect for me,
And with that, there was our future which I wanted to see.

A vibe so real of forever, a vibe so real about love,
And a vibe of home, a perfect home for a lost dove.

But the moment left when you could feel the same,
The day when I could finally be with you, my home.

A wish I prayed to god to "BE MY HOME" forever,
A place called heaven which I would never leave, never.

EROS

IF MIND AND HEART COULD TALK

"Inspired from a quote by ISHA GORASHIYA,
"LOVE SOMEONE WHO LOVES YOU, NOT THE ONE YOU LOVE""

MIND: I know you love her so much but just think if you will tell her, she might even end friendship.

MIND: She is a whole different world. So don't chase her. Please, don't mess things just be her friend.

HEART: If I could think, I would have been you.

HEART: All I know is Love and Pain.

MIND: But logically, she still loves him. She is finding him or his shadow in someone, while I don't want to be like his mind, the one who would break a heart.

HEART: But why I'm not lovable? Why him?

MIND: Now a day, many eyes aren't capable of seeing the inner beauty. All they can see is outer look and that defines love these days.

MIND: No one wants a caring and lovable heart. Maybe you are useless for this upcoming generation.

HEART: Maybe you are right but I would still beat for them till the time I can.

HEART: The world is becoming selfish that doesn't mean even we have to?

MIND: Want we are, is all because of soul! It defines what we will be.

HEART: Just for the sake of soul, let me express everything. Stop being my guardian.

MIND: Why do you want to put the gun pointer towards yourself?

MIND: She will not understand that it's her shadow whom you have started to love. It's her who defines everything to you.

HEART: All I want is that I get one chance to express my love.

HEART: Why won't her Heart fall for the love I have been endlessly waiting to express!

MIND: I don't want you to break again, that's the reason I don't want you to express her heart everything.

HEART: I will be fine if her heart wants to beat for someone else.

HEART: Please just let me try for once.

MIND: Okay fine. Go on but if you would be broken again. You will do as I say.

HEART: I would do anything just to let her know the truth.

HEART: I do know what you want me to do? Never start loving anyone again? But trust me there is nothing I can do about it

MIND: No I do know that there is nothing you can do about it.

MIND: All I want is "You Love someone who loves you, not the one you love."

MIND: Just like I gave a chance to express your love. I want you to accept the love if anyone is offering by giving it a chance too.

HEART: I could never think that, maybe because I can't think like you.

HEART: Now when I know that every heart needs a chance to express their love. I would definitely give a chance to everyone.

MIND: Just a warning that other minds may think and insult us for being with a lot of girls.

MIND: Wish you luck. Let's see if her heart and mind thinks the same. Do your best.

HEART: Thank you so much for always guiding me and proving me everything to work well and beat properly.

"Every heart needs a chance to express its love, make sure you give a shot/try"

WHO WINS? HEART OR TEMPTATION

TEMPTATION: Hey love!

LOVE: Hi temptation!

TEMPTATION: I still wonder. Don't you get Jealous as most of the People consider me as you?

LOVE: Not really. Because I am love and in love there is no space for jealousy.

TEMPTATION: Yeah! But people do have jealousy. Just like I do!

LOVE: Not all of them. There are many people out there who know what love means.

TEMPTATION: There are even many who can't even tell the difference between us! As they consider us the same. You should be shame of yourself. You can't even make people understand what you really are!

LOVE: You talking about shame? What do you do? You make people believe that it's me while it's you. There is betrayal when you come between two people. You make them go through the worst.

TEMPTATION: I don't regret being shameful because I come with ego. I then make an atmosphere that people feel that it's love. I try to change their attitude. I make them change one-another. I create Jealousy between them so they can end up in possession. Or else I make one betray another. That's how I make myself happy.

LOVE: Just because of you, people end up hating me. But still I can't get angry on you because I don't have anger as my quality.

TEMPTATION: People will never know your goodness! I will keep them in an illusion of love. I will make them hate you so much. You will have to end soon between people.

LOVE: There is one thing about me that maybe you don't know! I am an infinite source. Once I am there between anyone. No one can end the LOVE between them. Not even you!

TEMPTATION: Well, how many people can get rid of JEALOUSY? Can people leave their anger? Will they leave their ego, envy and rapacity? You will never be able to make people rid of these qualities because most of the people live on it.

LOVE: Most of the people do not include all people. Once people will know the difference between us, they will try getting rid of these qualities.

TEMPTATION: You dream so well! Keep dreaming! I have a better plan for people. Soon people will go through the darkest nights! They will have anger in their blood. They will get jealous of everyone. Their ego will not let them apologize to anyone! When they will greed for love! I will convince them that I am love! Well, I am not going to tell you the end, you better watch it yourself!

TEMPTATION: It would be fun watching them break apart. Well, it's not just the end of relations, it's your end!

LOVE: I know you are angry on people, jealous of me; your ego doesn't let you apologize for your crime! Your attitude doesn't want you to lose. You are scared if you will exist! Your greed of becoming "ME" will never end!

LOVE: You were talking about end of relations! Well, go on, you will never succeed because I believe in people! I still believe you can be better!

TEMPTATION: You are foolish! No matter how much you know me. I am going to succeed for sure. I am going to end you! Soon, I will be love!

TEMPTATION: My first step towards the end of you has already been successful. The fear among people to trust anyone is your first loss! Now, I am going to begin the second step of bringing jealousy between them which will be useful to create anger!

LOVE: I wish you the best but don't dream of replacing me because I don't want your dreams to tear you apart.

TEMPTATION: You wish for me? I don't need any of your stupid greetings! Keep on saying but I know very well whose dreams will break! As you wished for me, I will return you the favor, may your end come after breaking all your belief and hope.

LOVE: I can't understand why do you want to give people reasons to hate you? You can be better!

TEMPTATION: I just don't want you to win. I will take the risk of hating me but I cannot make you the winner without even fighting!

LOVE: It is not a game. Here we are dealing with the life of people and their feelings.

LOVE: I am already a loser; being love still I could not remove all your Aggression, Jealousy, Fear, Ego and Envy!

TEMPTATION: It is a game and I am going to make you a LOSER in the game as well. People will have to pay for creating me and I am going to make them suffer for it.

LOVE: It was not their fault! If you are considering it as a game then let just leave the game on people, we will wait and watch what people want in their life.

TEMPTATION: It would be easy for me! I am already among many of them. Then you will lose for sure.

LOVE: Let people decide about it.

Well, this does not End here. You all have to make a choice.

SMILE

Keep it real,
It will heal,
Just close your eyes and feel,
The power it has, to make everyone kneel.
Just smile, because it is weapon to kill.

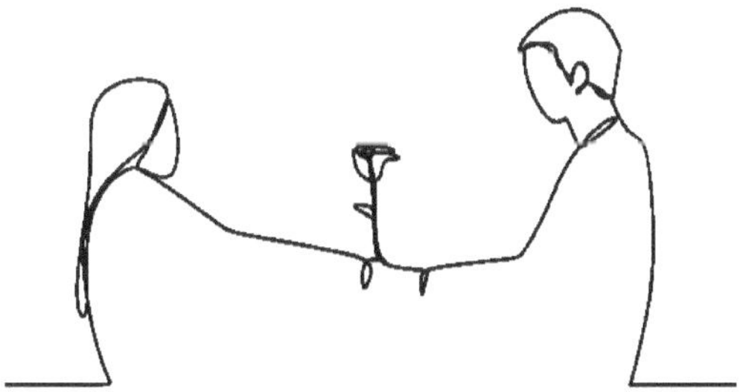

A Purest Soul

A purest soul,
Which makes me whole,
Stays with me in all my falls,
With whom I don't need to create a wall,
As there is nothing left between us that was untold,
Now just waiting for that time to fold,
Where she is doing my wife's role!

FAKE IS THE NEW TREND!

People come in life,
Few are fake, few are real,
Some have heart to feel,
While some have minds to use,
Who don't care whomever they lose,
Going each day ahead, it's becoming a trend,
It's because people lately show what they intend.
A world full of fake people, I learned keeping a fake smile,
And with that there was pain, following me right every mile.
A fake smile is where you start becoming fake my friend,
So keep trying it real in a world where fake is the new trend.

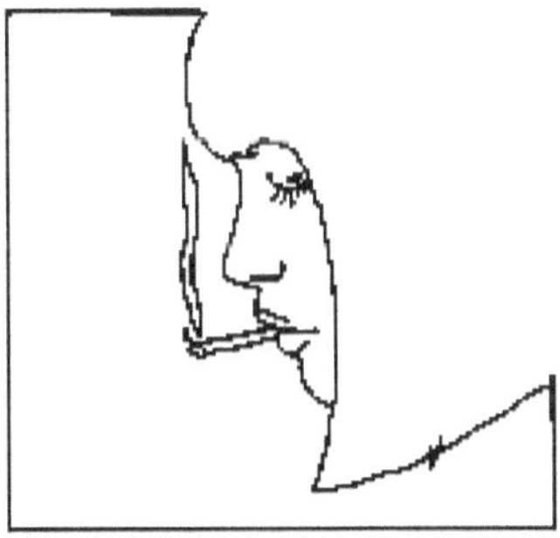

"BE MINE"

Be my FRIEND right till the END.
Be my BREATH till my DEATH.
Be my HEART without being APART.
Be my TRUST which cannot RUST.
Be my WAY for EVERYDAY.
Be my SMILE for every MILE.
Be my LIGHT even in the DARKEST NIGHT.
Be my KNIGHT to my every FIGHT.
Be my SOUL which makes me WHOLE.
Be my BEST and leave the REST.

WOULD YOU BE MINE?

She asked
"Would you love me? Would you be mine?
Because I want you, so bring that day that time,
When you are mine and it's just more than fine,
Because our love just finds a way to shine,
Please, let it shine and tell me if you will be mine?"

I replied
"I would love you because you are just mine,
I just want you every now and then, every time,
Every day and night, just to make my life fine,
With you and it's you who make our love shine,
So I should ask you, would you please be mine?"

THE TRUTH ABOUT US!

They said
"You won't have her, even if you wait,
Instead, understand that you're just late!
Or just ask her? For love, just say it.
The truth will break you and your faith,
Not yet, just wait for it, for that date,
For the end, you will blame your fate."

And I replied
"Even if I don't have her after I wait,
Instead, I will think it's never too late.
I will ask her for love and even say it,
The truth she will say, will keep the faith,
That maybe it isn't yet, it isn't that date,
For the end, she will prove that she is my fate!"

LUDUS

A LETTER TO DAD!

Hey Dad,
There are many things, which I have never expressed,
Like being your son, makes me feel I'm blessed.
From the time, when you kept your finger between my palm,
Waited so calmly, just to hear a "DAD" from my first talk,
And kept that finger, when you started to teach me to walk!
It was and will always be the safest hand to hold,
We both know, these are things which we have untold.
Just like sun sets every day, you made my dreams a way,
Worked too much, just to fulfill everything we want,
Then motivated me, when I lost to some fights,
And freed my fear when I was terrified by the nights!
Scolded me to make a better reflection of you,
And never let the light inside me to get dim.
To all the efforts you took for us,
I promise, I will equalize them by making you proud,
And that day I'm definitely gonna speak this letter loud.

A LETTER TO MOM

Hey Mom,
You already know everything which I never express,
All my secrets and all the reasons why I speak less!
Our journey starts right from the day you had me,
Your love for me didn't have to wait for you to see me.
All those pain through which you had to go through,
And saved me when there were things which I screwed!
Everyday working so hard for us without any break,
And all my favorite delicious food which you make,
A big thank you for everything that you have ever done,
And a sorry for not obeying you and taking stuff in fun!
Truly,
Your love and sacrifice can never be replaced by anyone,
You are just too perfect as a mother, there is no one like you, none.

A LETTER TO SISTER!

Hey SIS!
Just know that you mean so much to me,
There is nothing else I would ask to be.
Being your BROTHER is something I will always wish for,
And being brother is lucky because it's about being your.
There are memories that I will never forget,
As it is with the best people I have got,
The love between us is always gonna glow,
As you are the greatest gift my Heart will ever know,
I can't really imagine my life without you,
So know that I truly love you, I really do.

A LOVER'S UNSEND LETTER (PART-1)

Hey Love,
I wanted to talk to you about something,
Just know that without you, I am nothing.
I have fallen for you very deeply,
And want to be yours, completely.
But maybe you aren't there in my destiny,
Still glad that I'm your friend and not an enemy!
As loving you in an either way, was all I needed,
But being with you never succeeded!
Just wished for your love in return,
Even if you don't, just be with me at every turn.
Because,
My love for you will last forever,
So don't you dare to leave me, ever.

A LOVER'S UNSEND LETTER (PART-2)

Hey Love,
Hoping that you got my first letter,
And now, you know my love much better.
It was hard way to walk on,
But I didn't want you to move on.
I did expect that you would reply,
Didn't know, that you would never even try!
Still I can't just stop trying,
Even if I have to end up crying!
I am not the one whose love will die.
Cause my love is never gonna say goodbye.
Because,
Somethings does not have a happy end,
Just like the journey of being your friend.

A LOVER'S UNSEND LETTER (PART-3)

Hey Love,
Know that, I am not leaving you at any cost,
So please be with me because I'm lost.
In a way of love where I shouldn't have been,
But it's the most beautiful way, I have ever seen.
I would have been happy if you were there,
Being a couple and making a pair.
But unfortunately, all this is just an illusion,
As my love was rejected without any confusion!
But I still believe there is always some hope,
As our Friendship has always been so dope.
I even know I am not the one you have been looking for,
But at least give me a chance and open your heart's door.
As I will always love you, no matter what!
Mark my words, even if time changes I will not.
Because,
Some relations are always meant to shine,
Just like the relation of yours and mine.

A LETTER TO SOUL!

Dear Soul,
With every heart break, I felt you were real,
Cause you were the only one trying to heal.
I even know nothing really worked out,
But still you tried your best, without any doubt.
Letting go wasn't really easy for anyone,
Especially when you truly love someone!
Still I managed to come over it because of you,
Cause without you, there was nothing I could do.
I even had to thank you for that fake little smile,
Which you bought to show people even from a mile!
And for the nights when you helped me stop crying,
Because healing me was the only thing you were trying.
For all those helps that you always provided,
Like stayed in every heart break and never got divided.
Thank you so much for everything.

A LETTER TO PAIN!

Dear Pain,
Not her, you are the reason which started me to write,
And you ended feelings for some, without even a fight.
Changing people and making them worse is what you do,
Why? Why don't you leave even when people ask you to!
Life is becoming harder for me to live,
And there is hope which you always give.
Please stop all of this! I don't want it to end like this,
I can't stay without love as it's something I really miss.
In this world, very few things remain forever,
And I'm sorry but it can't be you, never.
You are something no one would ask for,
And none of us want to be with you, not more!
Because,
Love is what really matters to me and not you,
So I hope that you understand my point of view!

ONE LAST TRY!

Hello love,
Life has always been so cruel to me,
And there is only one thing left to see.
I even know you don't see me that way,
But let me clarify everything today.
I have started falling in love with you,
With that smile and those talks too!
Your smile is my last hope to smile again,
To feel happiness and free myself from pain!
How do I tell you what I feel? Where I'm?
A struggle of walking alone in the Darkness,
Searching for Light of Love, till being hopeless!
Hitting walls in the dark and losing hope,
And trying a last time, not to hear a nope.
The only chance for the ocean of love,
With the rain of happiness and joy!
A place which need a path to reach,
Holding hands in the path of each!
If you agree to be a part of it,
If not there will be love which I will quit.
"ONE LAST TRY" to convince to believe in my love,
Trying "ONE LAST TIME" to keep my love above!

MANIA

A THOUSAND YEARS!

I just think about you, every time I listen this song,
Why is it so? Why thousand years doesn't seem so long?

I guess because true love doesn't really end,
And so time feels short, no matter how much time we spend,

And it's always worth it, even if we spend it fighting,
Because life is just about you which is really exciting!

A journey from "The Day we met" to "A Thousand Years".
It was all about loving you and to our love "A Cheers."

Coming "One Step Closer" to you actually didn't stop,
Honestly I even wanted to, It was the only thing I hoped.

I know listening this song sometimes brings you tears,
But believe me some love is meant to last for more than
"A THOUSAND YEARS."

"PERFECT"

When "I found a love, for me"! I was glad it was you,
A girl who was "Beautiful and sweet", with whom I grew!

Being "kids when we fell in love, not knowing what it was",
All I knew was to "Give you best time" and then make it pause.

And telling you "Darling just kiss me slow" when we grew up,
As it was "Your Heart that I owned", kept in my heart's lockup.

"Baby, I, Dancing in the dark, you between my arms",
Where you were just slaying without any physical harm!

And "When you said you looked a mess", a truth so bright,
That it made me say "Darling you look PERFECT, tonight"

TREAT YOU BETTER!

It was never just about treating you better than him,
But to also keep you happy and smiling, without him!

And to make you understand about having a gentleman,
Because that is what you deserve and not a brutal man!

Everything was just so clear; he was bringing you tears,
Which I never would, I would never do that to you dear.

He did put fear in you when every time he beat you,
While that would have never been my way to treat you!

Because I would always, treat you better than he can,
And would have given you everything like a gentleman!

Because I know I can treat you better, better than anyone,
So all I'm asking is to come with me leaving everyone.

Just to treat you better! And make everything so better!
Before it gets too later! Because I know I can treat you better!

TWO OF US!

From deciding to live "One life for the TWO OF US",
There was no doubt in our love to be ever discussed.

From making me believe "day by day, not to give up",
It was only you who gave my life a purpose, a backup.

"Diamonds, they don't turn to dust or fade away,"
Just like them, you will always be in heart to stay.

"I'll keep you day and night, here until the day I die",
And meet you in heaven after telling this world our bye.

"I will be the best of me", I promise you that,
Because you were the Best in life, I ever met.

"One life for the TWO OF US", to again live it soon,
With all the love again, just like the love of sun and moon!

SEE YOU AGAIN

We've come a long way from where we have begun,
And this journey with you is just irreplaceable, man.

Cause it wasn't only about friendship but brotherhood,
And all those times when I needed help and you stood.

A never ending bond, never ending journey of two brothers,
And never ending love, a bond incomparable to all others!

From the time we met to the time we will meet again,
It's been so special being your brother, a gift I gained.

A gift which I will even follow to hell, without any pain,
Or even heaven, just to be there and "SEE YOU AGAIN".

F.R.I.E.N.D.S

Not just a show of six people and their friendship,
But a journey of their life and a bond that they keep!
Not just a show about the importance of friends,
But a love story of Ross and Rachel, with a happy end.
Not just a show about joey's food and chandler's jokes,
But showing their brotherhood, never to be broke!
Not just a show that contains a lot of happiness,
But also Monica's neatness and Phoebe's madness!
Not just a show around their jobs and their dreams,
But a world made with the Best Friendship Theme.
Not just a show to watch but an emotion to feel,
A lesson to learn, FRIENDS are always there to heal.
A Show which can be watched, over and over again,
Because it delivers emotions', needs to be gained!
A Show which made us cry when it came to an end,
Because moving on became hard for us without FRIENDS.

TILL THERE IS "HOPE"

Why is there always some hope left?
Or is it hope? which has got obsessed.

I would have tried to live my life without it,
I know it's impossible, I do admit.

There can't be a life without hope,
Because it's something, people need to cope.

A hope, to again have you and your true love,
Which till now you never really showed.

A hope, that she would say yes,
Praying a lot to god, to make this bless.

A hope, to get someone really faithful,
As been with one, who made life so painful.

A hope, that heart might get fix again,
With the power of love, that it would gain.

Hope! Hope! Hope! Of being all the way together,
Even though knowing, we can't be one forever.

Hope has kept us alive, as it is endless,
And so should be love, as none of us are heartless.

PHILAUTIA

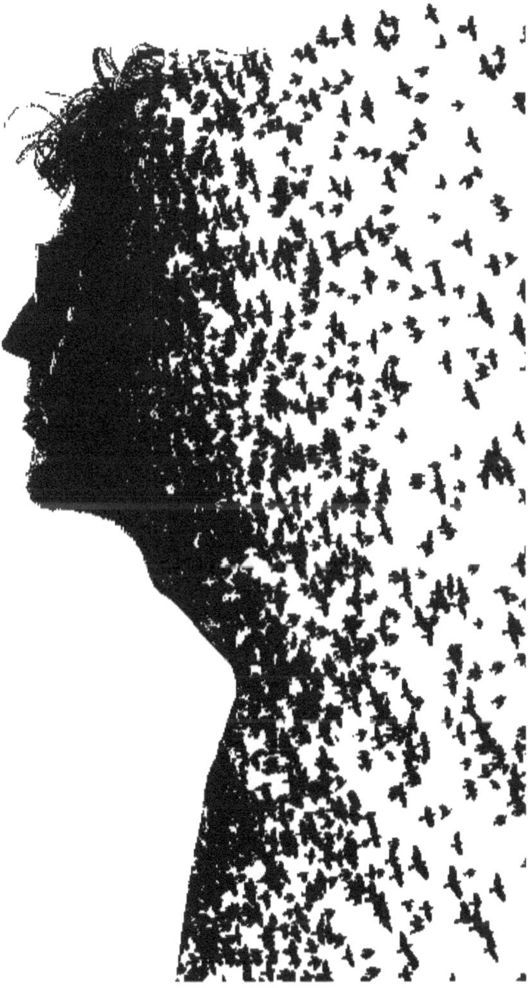

"SHE"

In the World full of Relationships,
I found a Friend who always beeps.

Talking with her on the call,
I understood we shared a beautiful soul.

Being misunderstood by the whole world,
Our friendship was like a piece of gold.

Living without her,
Was like portrait without blur.

Looking into her eyes,
I could catch all her Lies.

Laughing at each other,
She cared for me like a mother.

Watching her tears,
I wiped them, forgetting all my fears.

We travelled a different journey of Life,
Where she was everything except for a wife!

Till death, everything we shared,
It was all because we really, really cared.

I WISH I COULD GO BACK IN TIME

I wish I could go back in time,
And make your every bit mine.

Re-live every moment again and again,
And be happy with all the love gained.

As I was one of those guy,
Who looked at you with a secret eye!

Didn't have words to speak,
But did carry a smile on my cheek!

Till that day, when finally had a talk,
When we were having a late night walk!

And that one magical night which just froze,
In which my hand was carrying a red rose.

Having a surround with light breeze,
And the time when I went on my knees!

You wore the ring and changed my life,
It was all just because you became my wife.

I wish I could go back in time,
And make your every bit mine.

"ONE SOUL INHIBITING TWO BODIES"

Remembering the memories that we made,
Every time it kept on making me sad.

Started by being your brother,
And tolerated you like no other!

The times when you took the blame,
And still remained being the same!

Taught me the lessons which I needed,
And cried for me when I bleed.

One thing which always made my mood,
Was sharing the plate and delicious food!

Even after having lots of fight,
We always did what was right.

Listening this poem, she would be proud,
But she couldn't be here, in this crowd.

I am sure that she will definitely smile,
When this poem will reach her, crossing miles!

I always thanked God for giving,
Such an irritating sibling!

IT ALL STARTED WITH EYES

The day under that bright little sky,
When I saw those irresistible eyes!

You didn't just become my crush,
But a way of life, in which I wanted to rush!

You did became my love at first sight,
And I felt everything was going be right.

Those hair which came upon your face,
Tucking them back always brought grace.

And your damn contagious smile,
Which I would follow for every mile!

I could picture every single thing,
Even the time when I became your King!

I always saw you in my dream,
And when it got over, all I did was to scream!

But Life did found a reason to live for,
All it wanted was you, more and more.

This all was going to happen for sure,
Or maybe it was our bond, which was so pure!

SOUL BROTHERS

Today expressing everything to you, mate!
As it is the right time, I would not do late.

Time passed but the memories never faded,
Instead more and more good times added.

Like those rides with you and those races,
Some were safe but some injured our faces.

Teasing you with the girl you hate,
Makes us laugh, till this date.

Hey! Don't get angry or else I will shout!
And all those names, secrets will come out.

Well, let's talk about something else,
Or else I would be bitten up by belts.

So going to the food bills which you paid,
Made me hungrier, till stop was said

Just hoping our Friendship never dies,
Instead it gets honored with a prize.

Remember that our bond wasn't like others,
Because we have always been more than BROTHERS!

ADMIRABLE NIGHT

That night when the sky was full of stars,
We were on a drive and I stopped our car.

At a place so perfect for a song to play,
We came out, as we wanted to stay,

The tape and headlight of the car was on,
And with that all our fears were gone.

We started to dance, looking into each other's eyes,
As we both knew it was filled with love not lies.

We kept on dancing for so long,
Time stopped for us but not the song.

Soon even the stars were dancing,
And everything was so romancing

Having you across my arms,
I kept looking to all your charms.

Slowly coming closer we shared a kiss,
Which both of us will always miss!

Being around you, holding your hand,
I wished that night to never end.

WAITING IN LOVE!

How long do I really need to wait?
Maybe this was my luck or fate.

A hope that lightens every single day,
And with it there are tears which I pay.

One thing which was not fair,
Was that you never even cared!

You could have given a chance,
But you didn't even give a glance.

A belief of having you in the end,
But maybe it was never penned.

You would never know what it takes,
Because all you can do with heart is break.

Was that easy for you? To be just blind,
Or was it love? That you didn't want to find!

Life felt useless, as you were the reason to live,
And then there was love which you would never give.

Tell me the truth, if you will ever have feelings for me?
As my love is locked on you & your love is the only key.

WAS A GOOD-BYE NECESSARY?

Why did you to end up saying a good-bye?
At least you should have waited for me to die.

It was too easy for you to say this word,
But for me you were my whole wide world.

All those fights were just a matter of time,
And we both know all those mistakes weren't just mine.

You couldn't just hold, that was really painful,
Not even on my love which was so faithful.

Just let it go, I wouldn't be able to talk more on this,
Cause the more I will talk, the more I am gonna miss.

A WISH TO DIE TOGETHER!

I remember our entire life that we have spent,
And dying beside you is what I expect in the end.

Every talk and every walk that we ever had,
Will be missed, which really makes me sad.

The way we redefined "LOVE" was the Best,
As Love captured our hearts and never left.

From the days when we were strangers,
And the days when we became heart exchanger.

Between all those moments that we ever shared,.
It was Love, which taught us how to care.

Every memory I remember was just of us,
With all the happiness that you had plus.

Now, the only thing left without any rather,
Is "A WISH TO EVEN DIE TOGETHER"

ALWAYS AND FOREVER!

The promise I gave you weren't just words,
Because it meant living life like love birds!

They start their journey soon after their birth,
To find the right pair, anywhere from the earth!

When they finally find their life in someone,
They live their entire life beside their loved one.

Keeping each other in front of their eye,
And flying together high above the sky!

Loving and living, the only thing to do,
Till the time, anyone die from those two.

The other bird doesn't choose to live anymore,
Instead it dies, so their love can be adored.

Well, their love doesn't end here,
They start their next journey right there.

A journey to start after death,
To waiting to have their next breath!

The love they share can't be explained,
It is something which can only be gained.

From a true loved one, this is so rare,
Because there are people who truly care!

It is hard to find someone who is perfect,
Whose love can never be affect!

Just remember,
If you come across someone like this, ever,
Promise to be with them for "ALWAYS AND FOREVER".

WHY WASN'T I ENOUGH?

Why wasn't I enough?
Or was living with me too tough?

Why wasn't leaving tough, instead?
Or breaking someone till dead?

Why? Why wasn't "US" supposed to happen?
Why did it change to "YOU BOTH"? Why?

I already made a world between those lies,
In which I thought we would be, till each of us dies.

All those promises that you gave,
And all the memories that we saved!

All those FOREVER, where just a bluff?
Just tell me, why wasn't I enough?

JUST BECAUSE WE ARE GIRLS

Why don't you treat us equally like boys?
Why are we used just like playing toys?

Why do you tell us to cover our faces?
While we know we aren't safe at any places.

Why do you all think that we are weak?
Is it just because we don't really speak?

Or because we always forgive you all!
Still you do things which make you fall.

Is all this just because we are girls?
Or you all can't digest that we all are precious pearls?

A WAY OF HEAVEN

Having a blindfolded lady as a symbol of justice,
Which defines a lot and one is not to do injustice.

Holding a scale to weight and a sword to fight,
To punish all those who didn't do what was right.

Just Fight! Fight for yourself, to redefine that symbol,
Instead of hiding in the dark and getting crumbled.

We live in a world where it isn't safe for you,
But that doesn't mean it isn't built for you.

The first one to start life was Lucy, a woman,
So this does make it your world, since then.

So stop being afraid of it, instead start loving it,
Once you will start fighting for it, man will have to quit.

A world which does have some monsters to have you,
With some angels who are always there to save you.

God has given you the power to carry life in your womb,
A power to bleed and with all this, he gave a power to fight.

At last, just remember your life will set examples for many,
So make your every move for them, "A WAY OF HEAVEN" for any.

A QUESTION TO GOD!

There is this one question in heart, I have been carrying,
Then there is you who has its answer, but not sharing.

Just a why? A Why to you for not making me selfish too?
Waited so long and still do just to hear the answer from you.

Don't even know if I ever will get an answer to this or not,
And then there are many people for whom I had fought.

But even they deceived me for their own benefits from their lives forever,
Which again left me thinking, why couldn't I ever be selfish? Why?

Burring this question in heart, watching people fade and leave,
A question without any answer, was what I started believing.

A question which might many would be asking to god and themselves,
A question which shows to be mean and do what's right for ourselves.

THE UNTOLD WORDS!

There are a lot of things, we have never told anyone,
And all those "UNTOLD WORDS" for that special one!

Somethings are better when they are not spoken,
Because telling them sometimes makes us broken!

Then why are they there? If they are not to be told,
When are all those words and feelings meant to unfold?

Why so many questions to very few words?
For something which means the world.

I have hid it from you and from the world too,
Just to tell all them once with an "I LOVE YOU".

ONE LAST TIME

I remember how my love life used to make me cry,
Convincing to believe in my love, until that "ONE LAST TRY"

And in that I found you, a best friend and a true lover,
Someone with whom I didn't need to keep a cover!

I remember those talks and all those times we spend,
Which bought us together for life, like a love story penned!

And releasing today, in our last few days left to live,
There are many things we need to do again before we leave.

Do them again to remember those days for "ONE LAST TIME",
Since the time I fell for you and prayed just to "BE MINE"

When "IT ALL STARTED WITH EYES" unknowingly,
And slowly, slowly with that our love started glowing.

When we both realized about "A PURIEST SOUL",
Which brought us closer and later made us whole!

Like those nights we spend, specially that "ADMIRABLE NIGHT",
Added a lovely memory, something for which many would fight.

Wishing our love to glow for "A THOUSAND YEARS",
Staying beside each other while dying with some tears!

And "A WISH TO DIE TOGETHER" holding hands,
And meet you again in the same way we did as a Friend.

Doing this over and over again, until like ever,
Cause my Heart knows it about "ALWAYS AND FOREVER".

A HOME

Hello love,
I wish to have the mornings with you,
I want to hear a reply with an "I love you too".
I wish to do the cuddling and kissing,
And tell me I'm the one, you are missing!
Keep you happy to see that smiles,
Travel the world, holding hands, crossing miles!
I wish to have all of you and give you all of me,
I want to dream with you and make the world see!
What having a home really means!

AGAPE

A LOST FRIEND

I thought our Friendship was meant to last forever,
Our boundless bond which I might not find, ever!

It was our mistake, thinking our friendship's end,
While we could have discussed like best friends!

Just think of our lovely memory wall, a master piece,
Then why can't there be love again and along it peace.

Can't we keep our ego's aside and be back where we were?
Because I miss you duffer, so please be my ink to fur.

To write the beautiful journey of life again,
To build the same wall above, leaving all pain!

A friendship which gave us memories and happy faces,
And a lot more, the bond without any races or cases.

Let's just come back again, complete what we dreamt of,
A Friendship till death, a selfless friendship with true love!

"LOVE ME"

Every time falling in love with someone you can't have,
And feeling as if nothing's left except for a friendship to save!

Somewhere we know we will go through pain every day,
Where love will be silent and only broken friendship will say.

Carrying all the pain in heart, with no way to split it out,
Only tears to hide and a fake sound of laugh which we shout.

Being around her, talking less than what you really feel,
Then there is a "LOVE YOU" which you often say to heal.

And then there is a heart which keeps on beating to say,
"LOVE ME" at least for once, even if you don't every day.

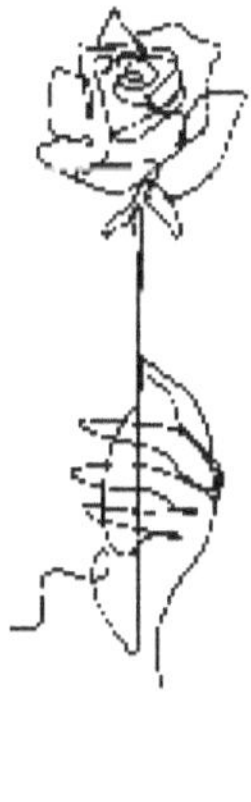

"11:11 WISH"

When you added that number behind those magical words,
It didn't keep anything left to express my love to the world.

A number which meant more, even more than infinity,
Because it wasn't about comparison, was about affinity.

Something that took our bond and our love to next level,
A relation so strong, no one could break, not even the devil.

Though those expressions didn't have meaning for many,
But all I cared was a reply I had to give you, better than any.

And that night at 11:11, when you asked for a wish and a reply too,
I replied looking those eyes "I love you 3000 too & will always do".

WHY I'M NOT HIM?

Everyday thinking the same thing over and over again,
Why I wasn't him? I would have got all her love to gain.

And all my heartbeats would have only been for her,
With those smiles which would have shined without blur.

And between all these, those love texts for making my day,
An 'I Love You' and 'Take Care' which she would always say!

And being possessive for me with a greed to have me all,
Hugs and kisses which I would share with that pure soul.

But knowing all this is an illusion, a life so damn dim,
No way to love her, just because I'm not him, I'm not him.

YES, I LOVE YOU

Yes, I do love you and I always will,
How do I tell you, what do I really feel?

Can't you see the love glowing in my eyes?
The purity it carries, free from those little lies.

A love as dark as night and as bright as sun,
And a sky like you completes the day, like none.

A love deeper than the oceans and seas,
Deep enough to put my world in your knees!

Why can't you see it and say? Yes, even I do!
And its only for you. Yes, I truely love you.

FOREVER WASN'T ENOUGH

Why did you do that? Why did you choose him over me?
Wasn't it hard? Couldn't you feel my love or even see?

Was it because I cared too much? Or I loved too much?
Did he love more than I did? Or was it the way he touched?

What happened that all your love lost faith in mine?
You told our love was forever and meant to shine.

Where did this eclipse come from? Where did I go?
Was it his looks? Or the money that you saw!

I always knew that the way of love is always so tough,
But never expected this, a FOREVER WASN'T ENOUGH!

A PROMISE, FOREVER!

Hello love,
Here is something which you always wanted to hear,
I enjoy every moment with you, so please be near.
Couldn't ever tell this but it's true, I love you madly,
And want to become yours and just yours, completely.
I want to hold your hand in every night during a walk,
And kiss you, making your mouth shut of those talks.
I want to feel you, this blessing in every way I can,
All smiles which you always bring, every now and then.
I want to see the world, I always see in your eyes,
Which brings light in my dark world, just like fire flies!
Between all this, I want to give you a really tight hug,
Want to travel the world, to every sand and every mud.
Grab me closer; hold me there, that's my happy place,
Cause there near you, all I can see is your lovely face.
Don't you dare to ever leave me, you get that? Never,
Because I promise it will be 'US', always and forever.

ABOUT THE AUTHOR

SHYAM KESHARIYA (BHAVIK) is a 20 year old, residing in Gujarat. He is a versatile writer, a poet and a lyricist. He is a first year student, studying IT engineering, from MARWADI UNIVERSITY. He completed his schooling from SAINT THOMAS, ATMIYA, UTKARSH and TAPASVI SCHOOL. Other than writing, his passion is photography and music.

He started with writing lyrics while now he writes quotes, poems, letters, and conversations too. Most of his work reflects love and "AN ELIXIR OF LOVE" *is collection of everything which he wrote on "LOVE" so far.*

He is the founder of "BE YOU" CLUB which currently conducts small open mics in his city, giving platform to other artists. He started organizing these events as his journey of becoming a writer started in an open mic too.

If you like his work and want to get in touch with him, you can email him on shyamkeshariya@gmail.com or can even contact him on social media networks @shyamkeshariya on instagram. You can even follow his pages @thenyctophilicponderer @be.you.club @time_snap_photography

ABOUT THE BOOK

"AN E L I X I R OF LOVE" *is a beautiful creation which is a collection of poem, letters, short conversations, quotes and write-ups based on different stages of love, such as friendship, romance, longing, procrastination, pain and even hate. With the beautiful use of words, I have managed to acquire all the emotions which a person goes through after falling in love. After reading this a person can cherish or rather experience all this emotions and most importantly can grow with them. This is a light, yet deep source for readers in teen-age or let us rather says the ones who have fallen in love.*

Readers would be able feel the unconditional love, the excruciating heart break, the procrastination about the longing from the dear ones and the rage caused by hate, after reading the book. It's a book which people would love to read and many would even be able to relate. It's a book which surrounds around love and shows the magic it has! It would touch your soul if you feel the emotions it carries. At last I would just say,

"EVERY WRITING DEFINES A STORY WHICH NEEDS TO BE HEARD".